Property

by Rosary Hartel O'Neill

A SAMUEL FRENCH ACTING EDITION

SAMUEL FRENCH

FOUNDED 1830

NEW YORK HOLLYWOOD LONDON TORONTO

SAMUELFRENCH.COM

ISBN 978-0-573-69760-9   Printed in U.S.A.   #18718

MUSIC USE NOTE

Licensees are solely responsible for obtaining formal written permission from copyright owners to use copyrighted music in the performance of this play and are strongly cautioned to do so. If no such permission is obtained by the licensee, then the licensee must use only original music that the licensee owns and controls. Licensees are solely responsible and liable for all music clearances and shall indemnify the copyright owners of the play and their licensing agent, Samuel French, Inc., against any costs, expenses, losses and liabilities arising from the use of music by licensees.

IMPORTANT BILLING AND CREDIT REQUIREMENTS

All producers of *PROPERTY must* give credit to the Author of the Play in all programs distributed in connection with performances of the Play, and in all instances in which the title of the Play appears for the purposes of advertising, publicizing or otherwise exploiting the Play and/ or a production. The name of the Author *must* appear on a separate line on which no other name appears, immediately following the title and *must* appear in size of type not less than fifty percent of the size of the title type.

PROPERTY was first produced in October 1999 in Thilisi, Republic of Georgia.

CHARACTERS

IRENE SONIAT DUBONNET: Sixty+. A landowner, she redefines the word style—in designer dresses, and flawless makeup. **IRENE** is one of those striking women—nerves of steel, iron lungs, sharp as a tack—who has nothing to do but protect her grown children, and she watches them like a dog guards her bone.

ROOSTER DUBONNET: (Nicknamed Roo) Thirties. A painter who has pushed himself beyond reasonable limits. He is critically ill. The disease gives him a distinct nonchalance, the charm of the damned.

BUNKY DUBONNET LEGERE: Early twenties, her grandson. He dresses like a rebel. His consuming interest is singing the blues. When he drinks, his personality changes into an exaggerated gaiety and a hair-trigger rage.

OOZIE RANSOM: Thirty to fifty. Companion to **IRENE**. **OOZIE** is always fixing herself—freshening her lipstick, puffing her hair, buffing her rings.

MONICA FALCON: Late twenties. A nurse, attractive, with a passion for things of the spirit. Delicate features match her gentleness: fine skin, graceful hands, hair which tumbles around her face.

SETTING

The day room of a Garden District mansion, New Orleans, Louisiana.

TIME

Valentine's Day to Mardi Gras. The not-too-distant present.

ACT 1

Scene 1

(SETTING: A spacious garden room. There is a luxuriously cushioned day bed with an empty bird cage like a Chinese house. Vivid landscape paintings are placed about. The effect is of a boy's dream, the actual furniture being less important than the wonder created.)

(AT RISE: It is raining quietly, one of those late afternoon showers that New Orleans is famous for. **ROOSTER DUBONNET,** *a young man, thirties, dark-haired, gaunt, almost emaciated, lies in bed in silk pajamas. If he were not so sick and pasty-looking, he could be handsome with strong features, thick hair, and broad shoulders. Even so, there are kindness and nobility in his face.)*

ROOSTER. If I could paint the rain—

(A knock at the door. He ignores it.)

MONICA. *(Off)* Hello! *(Another knock)* Anyone here?

(ROOSTER puts down his painting. Rain intensifies.)

MONICA. *(Off)* I'm coming in!

(MONICA FALCON, a nurse, twenties enters. Striking features contrast with her plain uniform and satchel. He gives her a hard look. Embarrassed, she studies her shoes and laughs.)

MONICA. These shoes look good before I walked through water.

ROOSTER. *(Rejecting her, mad)* Click your heels and go back to Oz.

1

MONICA. I'm **MONICA** Falcon, the—

ROOSTER. *(Calls out, angry)* No woman's going to undress me, look at my—

MONICA. The other nurses wouldn't come! You haven't been treating—

ROOSTER. Kindly leave!

MONICA. *(Entering)* What a wonderful home. It's like a hotel.

ROOSTER. *(Anxiously)* You're not staying.

MONICA. A block long mansion in the Garden District—

(MONICA puts down her bag, glances at the rainy window.)

MONICA. It's raining and there's this big bright sun behind it. *(MONICA goes to a table with medicines.)* Oh, here are your pills and charts. *(MONICA scrutinizes a bottle)* You can have... *(Stops herself.)*

(ROOSTER grimaces and leans to the intercom)

ROOSTER. *(Into the intercom)* Somebody pick up.

MONICA. Everyone's gone.

ROOSTER. *(Into the intercom)* Answer, I said.

MONICA. The butler locked up and left.

(MONICA takes out her supplies.)

ROOSTER. Don't unpack! *(Into the intercom)* Hel-lo.

2

MONICA. My art therapy class took a virtual tour of your grounds.

(He looks at her uncomfortably.)

MONICA. Where you painted the ancient magnolias, the bearded oaks.

(She crosses to him. He clutches his sheets about him, awkwardly.)

MONICA. I memorized your quotes from the Philadelphia School of Art.

ROOSTER. No closer.

MONICA. Some artists don't do interviews, and thank God they don't.

(She tries to take his blood pressure. He pulls the sheet over his head.)

ROOSTER. *(Peeking out)* Don't touch me. You're not hired.

MONICA. Why have you had no gallery shows . . . since the Whitney?

(He pulls down the sheet, looks at her aghast, reaches for his phone, dials.)

ROOSTER. Excuse me.

MONICA. Let me take your pressure.

ROOSTER. No. *(Referring to the phone)* Ah! Busy.

(She tries to feel his forehead.)

Stop! *(He redials)*

MONICA. Have you got a temperature?

ROOSTER. No. *(Grimacing in pain, to* **MONICA***)* Away! *(Into phone)* Visiting nurses? This is Rooster Dubonnet. *(Clears his throat)* I don't want this Monica Falcon.

MONICA. You remembered my name.

ROOSTER. I asked for a male attendant—What about Ludovic? Bill... No I didn't insult him. Sometimes I use the servants' entrance. *(Into phone)* I didn't scream at Roberto. They've got to speak English. The last attendant was stoned and talked all night on his cell. The one before threw a party upstairs.

*(*MONICA *snatches the phone, speaks into it.)*

MONICA. It's 4:59, Frank. Clock me in at 5:00.

*(*ROOSTER *reclaims the phone.)*

ROOSTER. *(Into phone, annoyed)* Hello! *(Coughs in pain)* Hel-lo!

MONICA. First, I'll change your sheets. Shall I help you—?

ROOSTER. *(Breathes anxiously)* Don't come near me.

MONICA. Well... rise!

(He stumbles to his feet, panting in pain, totters.)

MONICA. *(Watching him)* You can do it?

(Wind shudders through the room.)

MONICA. Stand by yourself? *(Pause)* I'm talking to you.

4

ROOSTER. *(Checks watch)* You have five minutes!

(Gasping, he pushes himself through the pain to walk away, stumbles.)

MONICA. *(Calls out)* Take my arm!

ROOSTER. I'm not some bag you can carry. . .

MONICA. Can you get to that chair?

ROOSTER. Out, Mephistopheles.

(He sets off a strobe light and siren. They fight for the siren. She wins, turns it off.)

ROOSTER. Out! Out! Looking me up. Trying to expose all my . . . I don't need some identity analysis student art therapist psychopath. You know how long it takes to paint blue like black.

(He stumbles to the chair, leans over the back, coughing, dizzy.)

MONICA. What pills have you taken?

ROOSTER. *(Checking his watch)* You have four minutes before—

MONICA. Can you keep anything down?

(He staggers. She crosses to assist him.)

ROOSTER. Don't touch me.

(Rain screams about. She pours him some water.)

MONICA. Take a sip.

ROOSTER. *(Checks his watch)* In three minutes, I'll press my panic--Have you heard of the nurse who poisons the emperor?

(Rain shrieks.)

This emperor so feared assassination—He only ate ripe figs from a tree. In the night, his nurse injected them with poison. In the morning, the emperor ate one and died.

(ROOSTER pours water on a plant. Grimaces in pain.)

MONICA. Mercury is in retrograde. So I'll excuse that behavior.

(She goes to him.)

MONICA. Let me take your temperature and I'll do your chart. My specialty is artists.

ROOSTER. *(Pushing her off)* I don't want your services.

MONICA. I took astrology in—

ROOSTER. It's amateur night in Dixie.

MONICA. *(Stubbornly)* You're a Virgo with a moon in Pisces—Which means you're sensitive. Right? *(Putting the thermometer in his mouth)* Your tenth house is Pluto in Leo. You're gifted at translating archetypal energy through the power of the personal image.

(He yanks out the thermometer)

ROOSTER. *(Cynical)* Are you from the South?

MONICA. Delaware.

ROOSTER. Y'all like to eat on paper plates in halls covered with graffiti.

(She tries to take his pulse.)

ROOSTER. *(Sarcastic)* What do you have going for you? Nurse psycho. That's what I want to know?

MONICA. My husband was from Jackson.

ROOSTER. *(Sneers)* There's a touch of Mississippi in your family? What does Mr. Falcon do—?

MONICA. My... late husband. Lord... I mustn't talk about— *(Wound up.)* It ... It's not professional... To be...

ROOSTER. *(Flustered)* Sorry. Do you need money for a cab home?

(Awkward Pause. She removes a folder, pulls up tall.)

MONICA. I haven't had time to study your files.

ROOSTER. Good because I don't need a real nurse. *(Checks watch)* Two minutes!

MONICA. The supervisor shoved this at me and—

ROOSTER. You're overqualified. The job is for a sitter. We have to use an agency because strangers steal.

(MONICA *is engrossed in the file. Her face falls.)*

(ROOSTER *points to the cage.)*

ROOSTER. Oh no. My parrot, Commander Butler, just flew in.

7

MONICA. Mmmm. You've had...

ROOSTER. Butler's my very special house ghost.

MONICA. Let's see—

ROOSTER. Butler can scream, "Where's the maid--And whistle, "Dixie." Calling the maid is so passé. Butler was bred by a gentleman who kept his plantation up river.

MONICA. You're in the last--

ROOSTER. I belong to the National Caged Bird Society, but I couldn't make that bird stay. *(Coughs violently)*

MONICA. *(Compassionately)* Case histories should be open to revision--

(Rain lashes about.)

ROOSTER. I may not have to land a plane on the Mississippi river, but something comparable awaits me. I've no interest in how soon I'll slide down the death pole. What do you know about painting? Looking up souls in a book. About critics, about the need to capture time? You'll not discuss my history, my paintings, my house. You'll not wash me, feed me, or water me like a plant!

MONICA. Good. I'll help you find that part of yourself that yearns for something spectacular.

ROOSTER. You're not hired!

*(A hard rain falls. **ROOSTER** stands with great effort. His legs wobble as his feet go numb.)*

MONICA. Let me help you to--!

8

ROOSTER. Back. *(Clenches teeth in pain. Checks watch)* One minute, and—

MONICA. *(Desperate, cries)* I'll level with you. This is my first assignment in Louisiana. I'm broke. I've been sleeping in my car. Let me do my job? Take your pulse, your temperature? I need this—It's the only 12-hour assignment. The rest are way—I could read you the news? Discuss art? Sit!

(ROOSTER has another cramp and sits. He tries to rise but can't. Ashamed, He looks down at his watch.)

ROOSTER. *(Checks watch)* 15 seconds!

MONICA. Are you in pain?

(Rain hollers.)

You sounded like you were in pain.

ROOSTER. Time's up.

(She crosses over, feels his forehead and takes his pulse. They eye each other awkwardly. Rain mounts.)

(Painfully, He stands and motions to the door.)

ROOSTER. Leave, and I'll pay you for 24 hours.

(She straightens the table, discovers the sketchpad, studies it.)

MONICA. Why have you had no shows... and quit creating--

ROOSTER. A week's salary if—

MONICA. When Degas went blind, he did sculpture.

ROOSTER. Okay. I'll pay you for a month.

(He shoves to his feet, totters, toes numb, then sits back down. Wind screams outside.)

ROOSTER. I've not stopped... because I wanted to... Today, I said, I'm going to paint, if my energy holds out...

(She gets a blanket and covers him.)

I'll get inside that rain and the wind screaming. Capture the cold blue in the morning. Bright blue at noon, Italianate blue now—... Rain's the pink lie. The last thing that popped out of Pandora's box with all her colors.... Listen to it blowing round. Coming through the trees... If I could paint the rain, the way it is, thick and smelling of oak leaves—

(Rain wails. She brings him the sketchbook.)

MONICA. I'll set you up in this chair, and you'll rise to the occasion. *(She opens the sketchbook)* You'll meet fate head-on, and from a brand new place-*(She points out the window.)* You'll create something extraordinary—. Like that cold bracing sunshine—Right behind the rain— *(She poises the brush in his fist.)* When you get too tired, we'll do as one artist suggests, tie the paintbrush to your hand.

(ROOSTER *raises the brush, takes in her energy, and starts to paint.)*

(MONICA *stands behind him as rain pours and the lights come down.)*

END OF SCENE 1

Scene 2

(The lights come up. Lapse of time of only a few hours. We are still in the day room. **IRENE DUBONNET** *enters in a smart contemporary cocktail suit with a hat and veil. She is holding a pistol and a purse. She yells off stage at her chauffeur,* **HUCK**.*)*

IRENE. *(Looks about)* Huck! Put up the car. It's dark as a coffin. I've seen funerals that were less solemn than this!

MONICA. I'm the new nurse.

IRENE. Huck, take down the rifles. Let out the dogs. *(Points the gun)* It's a trick to scare off burglars. *(Puts the gun in her purse)* I keep guns 'cause I hunt doves. I go to Mexico, shoot doves, and give them to the peasants.

MONICA. Strange hat.

IRENE. *(Looks in the mirror, removes a veil)* I get red if I even think sun. *(Glances out a window)* Whose rattletrap car is that? I don't know anyone who drives a Chevy.

MONICA. Mine.

IRENE. *(To* **MONICA***)* You should park on the Avenue. I can't park there. Last time, somebody smashed my windshield, and my insurance doubled. New Orleans is the worst managed and most—

MONICA. Intoxicating city. Before I came South, I thought flowers were—

IRENE. Where will you stay?

MONICA. I don't know.

IRENE. There's the servants' quarters in back.

11

MONICA. Thank you.

IRENE. *(Giving her the once-over)* You look like you just graduated from nursing school.

MONICA. I was twenty-eight yesterday.

IRENE. *(Looking back over her shoulder)* Ah, twenty-eight! *(Smiles)* Sit down. The chair for the nurse is over there. *(Pause)* What's your success rate with your patients?

MONICA. He's my first.

IRENE. You should always say it's your second. At least your second. *(She looks out the window at the dogs, yells)* Huck. Let out the dogs. Huck calls our house the dog spa. It's the Red Door of dog care.

MONICA. Tell me about your son.

IRENE. Roo's a fifth generation from the Garden District. Is it of any value, his rearing and education? This complicated system of breeding only understood by the sophisticated. Males here think as females in the fact they think a lot. *(Pause)* He's stopped eating. A bite of lettuce, a tomato but no meat.

MONICA. What's the patient's history with... ?

IRENE. He collapsed in Puerto Vallarta after painting seagulls on the beach.

(MONICA makes a note.)

IRENE. I learned one thing in this family. Watch art, don't be in it.

MONICA. Why has Roo stopped painting?

12

IRENE. They say you always stop when you're the strongest. I'm a secondary character in Roo's life. Most men are aliens...narcissistic, ruthless. Loving a gender they have been taught to devalue. What can we expect?

(IRENE exits to dogs barking. It is dark. **ROOSTER** *is asleep.)*

(SOUND: The clock chimes.)

(LIGHTS: Shadows creep across the room.)

*(*MONICA *turns on Bach music [something like* The Goldberg Variations, Three Part Invention, French Suites *or* Italian Suites*], lights the lamp.* ROOSTER *wakes.)*

ROOSTER. Have I been asleep long?

MONICA. Two hours.

ROOSTER. Why didn't you wake me? I'm embarrassed.

MONICA. Sleep's good for you.

ROOSTER. You should've waked me.

MONICA. Come see what we've got. Fresh strawberries. Happy Valentine's Day.

(He rises. Walks slowly to the table.)

ROOSTER. Valentine's? Is it?

MONICA. Cranberry juice?

ROOSTER. Not thirsty.

13

MONICA. Yogurt.

ROOSTER. Not hungry. *(He cries)* I'd hoped I'd feel better.

MONICA. You look stronger.

ROOSTER. Maybe later I'll go out.

MONICA. You're unstrung?

ROOSTER. I've been weepy a lot. You think it's the weather?

MONICA. What'd you do all day?

ROOSTER. I listen to the rain... Sage blue rain. It's beyond rich, beyond blue. Time loses its shape, the sounds glide, you feel time like rain... like...

MONICA. *(Picks up* **ROOSTER**'s *photo lying face down)* What's this?

ROOSTER. I played football. Quarterback at Jesuit. They used to say I was tough.

MONICA. Eat something.

ROOSTER. No, thanks. You know what bothers me most? The quiet...

MONICA. These strawberries smell good. If I cut one up, would you eat?

(He nods. **IRENE** *enters and sits* **ROOSTER** *up with a pillow.)*

IRENE. You should be resting, son. I'm having Mother's mink made into pillows.

14

ROOSTER. *(Turning away)* You didn't do that for me. I hate fur.

IRENE. Who told you to set the table?

MONICA. I wanted to help.

IRENE. Don't do anything till I tell you to. *(To* **ROOSTER***)* Dinner's late. Angela forgot to defrost the roast.

MONICA. Can I do something?

IRENE. Perhaps you can help in the kitchen.

ROOSTER. She's a nurse.

IRENE. *(To* **MONICA***)* I expect you to clean, mop, and sweep. You're responsible for Roo's area.

ROOSTER. *(Calls out)* I can do it.

IRENE. *(Shivers)* Don't be foolish... It's spring in the South. But inside, it's pneumonia alley. *(***ROOSTER** *has a twinge of pain)* I've got to wear a coat and keep the room at sixty degrees. So many layers. Makes me feel like a bird. I come prepared to shed.

MONICA. Snakes shed, birds molt.

IRENE. Don't you understand polite behavior? The phrase I prefer is "I agree."

ROOSTER. Oh-oh... a pain.

MONICA. *(To* **ROOSTER***)* You need help?

ROOSTER. Just your hand.

IRENE. Is this some new-fangled therapy?

15

(BUNKY LEGERE, twenty, dressed in black leather, struts inside balancing mail and a book. Afternoon champagne makes him defiant.)

BUNKY. You look wonderful. You look like a Queen. If I were a stranger, I would propose.

IRENE. *(Looks BUNKY over, doting.)* Those boys from Jesuit. Once you take them out of khaki, they don't know how to dress.

BUNKY. I began with the jacket. Then I went for the whole look.

IRENE. *(Affectionately)* There's something unsettling about having a mortician for a nephew.

MONICA. Nephew?

BUNKY. She doesn't like the word "grandson."

IRENE. Miss... Falcon. *(With adoration.)* Bunky Legere. It's not short for anything grand like Beauregard.

(Trying to lighten the mood, BUNKY plays "Goodnight, Irene" on the stereo. He and IRENE dance. ROOSTER rises slowly, takes a step or two and grabs on to a chair.)

ROOSTER. He sure can move. Everyone wants to catch him in a bell jar. Want to dance, Monica?

(ROOSTER dances with MONICA... both hit by love...then he falls.)

MONICA. Need help?

ROOSTER. No.

16

(He dances again, falls.)

IRENE. Huck! *(To* **ROOSTER***)* Son, what's gotten into you?

BUNKY. He's not hurt, is he?

MONICA. Nothing's wrong with him. He fell but he got up.

IRENE. Bunky, go clean Roo up in the bathroom.

(BUNKY *and* **ROOSTER** *exit)*

(She stops by the refrigerator) My second old-fashioned. Two's my limit. That's not what you'd call lapping it up.

OOZIE. *(offstage)* Angela's come. Dinner's in half-hour.

(IRENE *checks her watch.)*

IRENE. That's **OOZIE!** *(Explaining to* **MONICA)** I hired a companion. The daughter of my mother's housekeeper. Now she's taken over my third floor.

MONICA. When did Roo last go out?

IRENE. Sometimes he makes it to the slave quarters. *(Savors her drink)* Course he doesn't go lately.

MONICA. That must be hard for you... to see him get worse.

IRENE. I keep a cheery face.

MONICA. Because I imagine the thrill of his success...

IRENE. If I'm not optimistic, I don't come out.

MONICA. And watching him make great art.

17

IRENE. Can you hand me that swizzle stick?

(*MONICA gives her the swizzle stick.*)

IRENE. In his profession you're a failure unless you're a star.

MONICA. What led him home?

IRENE. *(Worrying about her drink)* More saccharine. (**MONICA** *crosses for a packet.* **IRENE** *shrugs her shoulders)* I don't understand his melancholy. I never had the luxury.

MONICA. Some people need to reflect.

IRENE. This glass is leaky.

MONICA. I'll get another. How did his depression start?

IRENE. First I thought it was the temper he'd shown as a boy.

(*IRENE checks the door to make sure no one is listening.*)

MONICA. Then?

IRENE. He began painting less and less. Before he was...

MONICA. Inspired.

(SOUND: Mendelsohn's "Andante Symphony no. 5" plays subdued.)

IRENE. Roo has always been special. *(Irritated, waves her hand)* Roo was born with a veil of skin over his face. A sixth sense. Nurse put it in a jar of formaldehyde.

MONICA. What did the doctors say... about his depression?

18

IRENE. They hit me with scientific terms for... the "C" word... Sent up these terminal statistics.

MONICA. Mrs. Dubonnet, you're crying.

IRENE. I'm not crying. I've an allergy. If you're done, go help the cook.

MONICA. Roo's life's still before him. He'll get better. You'll see.

END OF SCENE 2

Scene 3

*(Lapse of only a few seconds. We are still in the day room. **BUNKY** appears in the doorway.)*

BUNKY. Have y'all seen a purple pencil with the name of a funeral parlor on it?

*(**BUNKY** searches about, paces to the liquor table, pours a drink. The following lines overlap.)*

BUNKY. There's a party in parlor B before the parade tonight.

IRENE. *(Loving concern)* Don't you have a paper to write?

BUNKY. My brain hurts.

IRENE. *(Truly caring)* I'm trying to steer you in the right direction.

BUNKY. I'm not a car. If you want to steer something, buy a Ford. Having you on my case is like being pecked forever by a duck.

IRENE. Why do you want to study the blues? There's no future with—

BUNKY. I need to major in something I like. Find my identity.

*(**OOZIE RANSOM** sweeps in with truffles and a box.)*

OOZIE. Cousin Irene. Cousin Irene.

IRENE. You insist on calling me cousin.

OOZIE. "Plain Irene." Sounds disrespectful.

IRENE. Take a vacation from personality and be bland for a while.

OOZIE. I'm looking for Roo to show him my dress.

IRENE. He's with Nurse du jour.

OOZIE. What do you think of my going-away suit? *(Twirling about)* It's Buck-a-roo blue. I'm getting a whole bedroom dyed this shade.

BUNKY. *(To OOZIE)* It looks very Renaissance.

OOZIE. Fin de siecle. My wedding's using a Victorian theme. See my invitations. *(Reads)* "Mrs. Peter Malter Dubonnet requests your presence at the marriage of her cousin."

IRENE. It doesn't say third cousin, or cousin-in-law.

OOZIE. Oh my God—a typo! It says Fl**OOZIE**, not **OOZIE**. God. *(Puts invitation to her eyes)* No, it's my contacts. *(Reads)* "To Purvis Axelrod."

IRENE. OOZIE Axelrod. Doesn't go together.

OOZIE. "Reception immediately following the ceremony, New Orleans Country Club." You have to be a member to entertain there. I told Purvis, "I don't want much for my engagement but I want it big and I want it real." *(Flashes her ring)*

BUNKY. Don't wear that on any back streets.

OOZIE. He keeps saying, "Where have you been all my life?" I reply, "Well, for half of it, I wasn't born yet."

IRENE. It's easy to flutter if your groom is eighty-one.

BUNKY. Poor Purvis...You have to tie a pork chop around his neck to get the dog to play with him...

(BUNKY exits.)

21

OOZIE. Purvis won't let me do a thing. The only exercise I get is to switch on the ignition, to press the air conditioner, and to dial the car phone. Without cars and the weather, there'd be nothing to talk about.

IRENE. What business is Purvis in again?

OOZIE. Purvis is a third-generation screw manager! He's gone further faster than anybody!

IRENE. It's awkward to say he's in screws.

OOZIE. He runs the family business, "The House of Screws." Forty thousand feet of screws... There are fifty types, Italian screws, French screws. He's got a ranch paid for by the House of Screws. Rooms and rooms of furniture and *(Pronounces it wrong)* tester beds.

IRENE. *(Correcting her)* Tester. If you were a first cousin, you'd know. *(*MONICA *enters)* Monica, meet Oozie Ransom. A distant relative of my late husband.

OOZIE. I was born Elvira. But I didn't like it so I had it legally changed.

MONICA. Monica Falcon.

OOZIE. Falcon? I don't want to be eaten.

IRENE. Ha. Now Oozie's leaving. The last person who knew my Mama.

OOZIE. I'll have eighty acres of Texas land and my own ranch, three blocks long. Purvis had the nerve to add on.

IRENE. A big house? At first, you do it, then it does you.

22

OOZIE. I found the right key and all the doors are opening. With one "I do," I'll go from tenant to landlord. I'll have three dogs: Quiche, Brandy, and Caesar, and look for people to do nothing with.

IRENE. I thought you liked it here?

OOZIE. Now I can enjoy the fruits of my labor, of all those years of hustling on tired feet, knowing the only excuse for not showing up for work was death. Mine. I'll learn to become soft in a house that's bigger than yours. The way to happiness I see is being a woman of property. With means, you can say things that cause flack. Property gives you courage. You can take that power and live it for the rest of your life.

IRENE. *(Stumbles, then screams, as they exit)* Why must Huck wax every step? Someone's going to trip and sue me for a million dollars. *(to* **OOZIE***)* Go check on dinner.

OOZIE. I never wear a watch. I don't know the time.

*(***OOZIE** *and* **IRENE** *exit.* **ROOSTER** *enters with a scented candle. He wears a fresh shirt and slacks.)*

ROOSTER. It's going to be a wet night?

MONICA. Yes.

ROOSTER. No moon?

MONICA. No.

ROOSTER. A splendid sky, wonderful, dark with three stars.

MONICA. You like having company.

ROOSTER. I like having Monica.

(**MONICA** *pours him water. Places it in his hand. He holds hers.)*

MONICA. Drink. *(He takes one sip; she watches him)* You lived at home for a long while? That's hard...

ROOSTER. Not if you need money and time.

MONICA. What was your mom like... before?

ROOSTER. Mom's a bravura figure. When you're fifteen years old and you think you can do anything, Mom is someone who can help you think you can do that. How wonderful Paris is, she'd say, and we'd be off with a maid to pack and a teacher to explain the tour. We would stand for hours before the Renoirs at the Louvre. *(Breathing deeply)* While she studied the light and the shadow. Then we'd take a few days off and go to the Baltic Sea. The National Gallery in London. Perganon in Berlin. We'd ride in taxis above the crowd... stay at the Ritz. It was the white-glove approach to travel... breeding children who reacted to a European sensibility. *(Pause)* I'm her last child so I ride on the cusp of her extravagance. *(Rain whistles around the house. Rubs his hands together)* Listen to that rain.

(SOUND: Rain howls outside.)

ROOSTER. Fix my blanket. *(She puts a blanket over* **ROOSTER***; he squeezes her hand)* Thanks. I'm afraid I'm going to die and never get off this bed.

MONICA. Listen to me. I'll take care of you.

*(***ROOSTER** *falls asleep.* **MONICA** *moves to a chair, sits, studying the report.* **BUNKY** *enters, chased by* **OOZIE** *and* **IRENE**. *The following lines overlap.)*

24

BUNKY. My report card. It's meaningless.

IRENE. *(Disappointed)* Between the Valentines! All F's for absence.

OOZIE. Why didn't you have an ugly friend say you were sick?

BUNKY. I've never taken a test. I refuse to be tested!

IRENE. I'm not traumatized. Not after last week. When Bunky wore spandex to Ferdie's. And got potatoes in his eyebrows.

OOZIE. How can he study, with girls out back till three a.m.?

IRENE. Beer cans lining the drive—

BUNKY. Like hell.

OOZIE. He gobbles aspirins.

BUNKY. Like hell!

IRENE. I could take a few exasperated screams, but to make "hell"—a part of the currency of conversation!

BUNKY. Music pushes your spirits up. Ka—boom. *(Singing)* There's a crying Blues. A three o'clock moaning Blues. *(Hits a high note)* That's falsetto. The deceptive voice. Nameless artists taught me that. Great unknown figures. Their families erased them after they died. If you distill Blues to a drop, it'd be a prisoner with a guitar and a hot toddy. *(Sings solo song and dances to a rap)* Hot toddy in the cool rain. I love to sit in the rain and let the sounds come through the bones of my body like liquid music. Be there like the Mardi Gras Indians that come out to dance in the drizzle. I'd forget who I was and say, "Something is right with this picture."

END OF SCENE 3

Scene 4

(Sometime later. **ROOSTER** *enters in a sweater and slacks, holding flowers behind his back.)*

ROOSTER. *(Hands* **MONICA** *roses)* Happy Mardi Gras. Do you know you've been here for thirty days?

(As **MONICA** *passes him, he takes her arm.)*

ROOSTER. You're a Dresden shepherdess.

MONICA. Don't forget to take your medicine.

ROOSTER. Light just kisses your hair.

MONICA. The light kisses me. *(She puts a thermometer in his mouth)* That's nice. I studied you in my astrology class. I'll give you the bare bones of it.

ROOSTER. *(Removing the thermometer)* I'm not ready.

MONICA. You've come out of the womb wearing female clothes.

ROOSTER. Preposterous.

MONICA. You are to grow towards the territory of world teacher.

ROOSTER. Too big a role for me.

MONICA. Your core assignment is to express the personal story through the universal medium. *(Shakes her head as she reads the thermometer)* Still this low-grade fever.

ROOSTER. I'm not taking on a personal assignment. *(Shudders)*

MONICA. You okay?

ROOSTER. Comes all of a sudden...

MONICA. Mind if I peek at these paintings? *(Picks up a painting)* This one looks like a holding place for heaven. *(Lifts another painting)* And this. My.

ROOSTER. *(Humiliated)* A tree is naked.

MONICA. Is someone selling these?

ROOSTER. *(Puts away the paintings, ashamed.)* I contacted the first agent for money, the next three for revenge... the fourth agent said, "These are highly marketable paintings. I suggest you show them to someone else." The fifth agent said, "I wanted to like your paintings, but I don't." The sixth was the cruelest. "I like the birds, the atmosphere, but there's no substance to the work." The last agent was triumphant in his rejection. "Painting the South isn't fashionable," he said. They say Southerners will always paint the South, but I didn't think I would because I always felt like an outsider.

MONICA. But you were born here.

ROOSTER. *(He has put up the paintings and sits exhausted)* Listen to that wind... I need a rainstorm every now and then.

MONICA. I had a passion once... for someone.

ROOSTER. Your husband?

MONICA. I was totally prepared for his death. I'll never be as prepared as that... and then when it came... when they put him in the ground, I thought this man who dominated my life doesn't live anymore. He gave me my ideas. I keep thinking of my husband lying inside his casket. When I went to choose the coffin, I was so broke I couldn't pay much. Now I'm glad I did. The lids of the

27

better caskets fit so well. I ran my fingers over the smooth gold trim. I thought about rain leaking in the casket, and I went and bought an expensive airtight one. You think when people look at a casket, they know how much it costs?

(BUNKY bursts in.)

BUNKY. Uncle Roo... I've got to talk to you.

(MONICA starts to leave.)

ROOSTER. Where're you going?

MONICA. To get a vase.

(MONICA exits.)

BUNKY. *(Madly in love.)*For God's sake, don't talk to Angela. *(Crosses for a drink, tormented.)* She's collecting all the sleeping pills she can find in the house. Gosh! She's three months pregnant. I could marry her. She'll probably abort the thing.

ROOSTER. No. This'll be a wealthy baby with a big inheritance. Rich babies don't die before they're born, but in a car wreck at fifteen. But poor Ma. Losing her companion, and her cook. When will you announce the news?

(BUNKY refills his plastic cup, exits. OOZIE enters.)

OOZIE. Dinner is ready. *(Notices the flowers)* Did Purvis send them? *(Reads card)* "I absolutely adore you." *(Exits screaming)* Cousin Irene. See my flowers. Cousin Irene.

MONICA. I saw your show in Philadelphia.

ROOSTER. *(Humiliated.)* Unlikely.

MONICA. Two years ago. *(Smiles softly)* I can't paint, I can't write, but I can recognize quality.

ROOSTER. After Philadelphia I quit. Soon as I did, people said to me, "You look liberated." And it was true.

MONICA. Your life was easier.

ROOSTER. No one hated me anymore. I'd spent my whole life bullying people into hanging my paintings. Watch out, it's him again.

MONICA. But you started as a legend.

ROOSTER. Successful, but on a shallow incline.

MONICA. People said your name with reverence.

ROOSTER. *(Self-hatred.)* Before they boiled me in a pot and ate me.

MONICA. *(Picks up a portfolio)* And you do everything: oils, watercolors, pen and ink. Oh... my... sketches of me. Well?

ROOSTER. Horribly awkward, isn't it?

MONICA. You haven't done your best... your finest...

ROOSTER. My signature work?...

MONICA. When you start painting a lot, it will happen.

ROOSTER. In my last painting, I sought the perfect blue. I thought of myself as being inside the blue...

MONICA. *(Opening an envelope)* What's this?

29

ROOSTER. I don't need any more slaps from the museum people.

MONICA. You do nothing, and they give you an award.

ROOSTER. I'm sick. Maybe I'll die.

MONICA. You're living now.

(He has a sudden cramp, staggers.)

ROOSTER. Something's wrong with me again...*(Holds on to the table)* I'm dizzy...

MONICA. *(Trying to support him)* Breathe.

ROOSTER. It's nothing. *(He stumbles to a chair, sits, grins until the pain dies down)* It's... gone.

MONICA. Lie down.

ROOSTER. How did this happen?

MONICA. It'll get better. It's simply hard now, after the treatment; trust me.

ROOSTER. That's what I believed. *(He has another weak spell.)*

MONICA. Don't talk.

ROOSTER. I've been thinking about the place I'd like to live with you. It'll have eight rooms, a wraparound porch, and beautiful trees... a magnolia, a pecan, and an oak.

MONICA. I don't think I could live in the South. I'm not a real New Orleanian. My great-grandparents didn't live here and bank at the Whitney.

30

ROOSTER. It's okay to be a Northerner for a while. *(Pause)* I haven't had many women in my life. That's the truth. Work and pain... I don't want to die.

MONICA. You're not dying. You're living. *(He relaxes and lies back on the bed)* You hear me? *(He closes his eyes)* Sleep.

ROOSTER. I want to talk about my paintings so you'll understand...

MONICA. Rest. My husband's name was Speed. He got that from playing football. He told me, "When I die, I want you to be there." We became closer through his disease. Suddenly, one afternoon he breathed a little moment and went away. It was just a breath, it was very calm. But you will not die. (Pause) Your life's your own, and you must do something with it.

ROOSTER. Don't leave me if I sleep.

MONICA. I won't.

(He closes his eyes. She watches for a moment.)

ROOSTER. *(Screaming)* Monica. Monica!

MONICA. What's wrong?

ROOSTER. I had a bad dream I was burning to death. I kept calling to you to save me.

MONICA. And did I?

ROOSTER. I don't know. I woke up. You don't think I'll die, do you?

MONICA. Probably not.

31

ROOSTER. Because I want to live till I'm old. If anything does happen to me, will you promise you'll take care of my paintings? Same as if they were yours?

MONICA. Same as if they were mine.

ROOSTER. Is it hot in here?

MONICA. No, honey. It's cool as evening.

ROOSTER. I want you to make me push myself to paint.

MONICA. I'd like to.

END OF SCENE 4

INTERMISSION

ACT II

Scene 1

(The day room. Three weeks later. Six p.m. The afternoon is drawing to a close. Something like Wagner's Lohengrin's Bridal Chorus plays on the stereo. A lighted lamp stands on the table. **IRENE**, *in a Victorian "mother-of-the bride's" dress, is sitting reading a "Town and Country" magazine.* **OOZIE** *is dressed in Victorian wedding attire complete with tiara and veil. She stands at the back of the room for a moment with her hands clasping a nosegay. Then she comes back near the table, picks up a mirror and looks at her face.)*

OOZIE. *(Imperious)* How do you like my dress?

IRENE. Pretty, but it's not soft enough for me. We've different tastes.

OOZIE. That's what I wanted. Purvis accepts me at face value. I don't want to look frail like I'm living in a fairy tale.

IRENE. You don't.

OOZIE. I just hate the way I look. I had my hair done. I liked it for about an hour.

IRENE. *(Looks at* **OOZIE**'*s hair)* Strange shade. Looks like chicken feathers.

OOZIE. It's my natural color so my hair's a restoration. Now I've passed the big four-oh I've switched from cheap barettes to a headband. And a Wonder bra..

IRENE. Big fifty, and you're pushed up too high!

33

OOZIE. Why are you nasty with me? Roo's the one you should yell at. *(Striding up and down the stage)* He's with that nurse. And what's more, she's not from here. She's an import.

IRENE. To think Roo was in "Life Magazine" at twenty as one of the red hot one hundred.

OOZIE. It's not just the photo but who takes it.

IRENE. But if your photo's not to the paper on time...

OOZIE. I will not get the upper right-hand corner of the Living Section. I know. I don't know if I'm frustrated or disappointed.

IRENE. You always have problems with distinctions. Frustrated is like an itch. Disappointed is like a tear.

OOZIE. *(Puts Irene's hand to her chest.)* Roo's giving me high blood pressure. Can you feel that...Ba-bump, ba-bump. Hear that?

IRENE. No. I smell my perfume.

OOZIE. Roo doesn't call home, if he doesn't feel like it. He doesn't know they've invented South Central Bell?

IRENE. Never do anything for men thinking you're going to get what you want. To be effective, one needs to expect catastrophe. This should be easy. I've watched so many boys in the Garden District acquire an unfeeling attitude. They stay at home but they aren't there except when they're tired, hungry, or broke. For entertainment, they torment their relatives. Women are by nature more sensitive than men. We've to curb ourselves to keep them. It's not their fault we're more intelligent. We provide amusement. We have for centuries.

(SOUND: The clock chimes.)

34

OOZIE. Fitting end to a lousy day. I'm going to get changed and drive myself somewhere nice. *(Starts to go, stops, and crosses to the phone, dials.)* Lord! I've no car. Purvis promised to lend me his.

IRENE. You drive a car until it smokes, and he won't let you do that to a Jaguar...

OOZIE. I hope his secretary's not using it.

IRENE. Already? These questionable generosities.

(IRENE returns to her "Town and Country," looking preoccupied. Awkward silence. OOZIE sits, yanks off her shoes, and sticks her feet out. Horrified.)

OOZIE. My feet hurt. I need a toe reduction. I just hate my toes. My second one's too long. *(Rolls her hand. Looks for ROO. Holds up her ring)* This is a two-carat diamond. It's very nice, but Purvis gave his first wife a five-carat flawless one from Tiffany's! She kept it after the divorce.

IRENE. You can keep yours, too.

OOZIE. *(Crosses and brings IRENE her drink.)* I'm not marrying Purvis unless I get jewelry of equal value. Purvis is not my dream man because he lies, steals, and cheats.

IRENE. Every man should have on his desk, "The truth stops here."

OOZIE. If only he would lie to other people and tell me the truth.

IRENE. They lie once, twice. Then lying becomes addictive.

OOZIE. *(Stuffs Kleenex in her armpits.)* I'm sweating like a pig!

IRENE. Ladies "moisten." They don't sweat!

35

OOZIE. Keeping myself intact is impossible. I've got to move in sections and reassemble once it's safe.

IRENE. I'd say things are fine, but they're not. Just like that summer you and Pete were in this house.

OOZIE. *(Clears her throat.)* You and Pete weren't talking except at the Carnival balls.

IRENE. You don't have to chat to be valued.

OOZIE. Pete was so easy, so good, so...

IRENE. Try not to talk so much, so we can live with each other.

*(*BUNKY *enters impatiently, hurries over to the liquor cart. He pours a fistful of aspirins and unscrews a bottle, and ignores* IRENE.*)*

IRENE. Another bird in flight. *(To* BUNKY*)* You didn't tell me, "Hello!"

BUNKY. I said "Hello" this morning when I saw you in the parlor.

IRENE. But is one hello a day enough?

OOZIE. He can't talk to us mortals.

IRENE. You get up looking for a drink?

BUNKY. I'm trying to kill this headache.

OOZIE. By mixing alcohol and aspirin!

BUNKY. I drink more when it rains. You, see, there's reality, and there's real reality, under everything else. If you get too much into real reality, you'll drink too. Salut.

(He pours himself bourbon and a glass of water.)

IRENE. I've nearly been ignored to death on some occasions.

*(The phone rings. **BUNKY** hurries back in. **OOZIE** grabs the phone.)*

OOZIE. *(Into phone)* Hello... Who? What? (To **BUNKY**) Ocshner Clinic. *(To **BUNKY**)* They hung up.

BUNKY. *(Terrified for Angela.)* I'm going to sit in the rain. I'm talked out.

OOZIE. Wait. Didn't I see you there? I was in a class, "Intimacy for Seniors."

BUNKY. I wasn't there.

OOZIE. Well, it must have a been a holograph of you!

*(SOUND: A phone rings. **BUNKY** grasps it and whispers into the phone.)*

BUNKY. *(Desperately.)* Hello. It's sure? Yes... yes...

*(**BUNKY** slips offstage with the phone. **IRENE** peers at the garden.)*

OOZIE. Finally the king arrives. I can't wait to give him my own hospitality.

*(**ROOSTER** and **MONICA** enter the garden whispering.)*

37

ROOSTER. Audubon's the most sensual park. Geese gliding in the ponds.

MONICA. Camellias. So big and light.

*(*ROOSTER *and* MONICA *enter through the garden door.)*

ROOSTER. Every time I go out I feel I can paint again. I'm a magnet for the color.

IRENE. *(Truly worried.)* You want to get worse? *(Points to the door)* You're throwing the cooling system off whack.

ROOSTER. I cancelled our sitting.

IRENE. How could you? She's afraid she's losing her looks, and there wasn't much to begin with.

OOZIE. Only someone heartless could fail to see how important a good photo is to a woman... nearly forty.

IRENE. *(Rises irritably.)* Fifty. Can you help the girl?

MONICA. *(Exiting)* It's Roo's choice, isn't it?

OOZIE. *(To* ROOSTER*)* I need a great wedding picture. I've had two premarital divorces.

IRENE. Don't cry and ruin your mascara. Just because you've been under the knife doesn't mean you're photogenic. *(Exiting)*

OOZIE. Yes, well... Your mother is a witch. Still, it's hard to leave. The big wonderful bedrooms. The polished Cadillac by the door.

ROOSTER. *(Angry at her.)* It was a good place to live from zero to eight.

OOZIE. We'd sit in the dining room, jingling our glasses, popping a pecan.

ROOSTER. I don't want to talk about the way it was.

OOZIE. OK. Good-bye, Saint Charles Avenue. Good-bye to the grand piano. And the garden. And cut-glass front doors... satin comforters sliding off your legs. Does anyone value New Orleans while they're living in it?

ROOSTER. *(Seething.)* Dad did maybe, he did some.

OOZIE. Sometimes I don't know if I was happy or miserable in this house.

ROOSTER. It could have been nice to live here... if we didn't have this cloud of uncertainty. When you and Dad were on the porch with that little light on, I'd go to the gallery and watch the streetcars clang by. And in her room Ma would sit up late, immobilized, the help grumbling in the kitchen. Dad and you. Just talk or fire. *(Pause)* I realize I was born as a last attempt to save their marriage.

OOZIE. I wished you were mine.

ROOSTER. *(Points outside.)* Look, the rain's cooled it off. Ma's cutting some flowers. I look like her. I never realized before how overwhelming she is... so much love and yet somehow a lie inside all the affection.

OOZIE. I never loved any other man. Can't you forgive me?

ROOSTER. Sometimes I think if my mother had the right loving, she'd be warmer...

OOZIE. Soon I'll be your aunt of, with, by, and from the state of Texas.

(IRENE enters)

(OOZIE exits)

IRENE. Oozie? What's wrong? Roo. Have you been tormenting
OOZIE?

ROOSTER. *(Suddenly confident.)* I wanted you to be the first to
know. I'm right next to a change, but not yet in it. *(Struggles with
himself)* Yesterday and again today, I told myself it's impossible...
Sit. Please. You ever notice how colors change and certain leaves
are lit up, darkness growing into light? *(He puts his hand to his
head)* I feel hope.

IRENE. Hope has been unfashionable for a long time.

ROOSTER. I know. When men leave, people see it as heroic, but
when...

IRENE. *(Affectionately.)* Be thankful you've a home.

ROOSTER. *(Proud.)* I thought I'd never concentrate again... not
like before. Then The Hyde Museum started hitting me with phone
calls—I got a grant. A year's retreat in North Carolina. It's one of
those rare miracle days that blow your mind. I'm going to travel
again. Paint my signature work. I can't do a miracle here because
I'm the son of the son of the son.

IRENE. Yes. You belong to a family who embodied the best of
tradition. What's wrong with that?

(SOUND: We hear a parade passing.)

IRENE. We'll talk this out later. Now let's watch the parade. I
added up the years our family has been involved in Carnival, and it
came to one hundred twenty-three. *(Points at the parade)* One day...
I hope... you'll dress like a captain, in white velvet with a cap and

40

plume. You'll ride horseback before the floats... then escort the queen in the grand march around the ballroom. *(Picks up a scepter and crown enshrined on a table.)* The Carnival Ball links the South with European culture. Your great-grandmother, grandmother, and I were queens—

ROOSTER. I am so fed up with this.

IRENE. When you're Queen of Rex, the doors of society swing open.

(SOUND: Jazz band from the parade.)

Remember when you costumed in Proteus ball—

ROOSTER. When I was ten.

IRENE. As the son of Paul Revere? Now you want to cut your very deep roots to the city?

ROOSTER. I need to separate myself...

IRENE. In time your paintings will disappear, but Mardi Gras and its traditions will survive.

ROOSTER. I don't believe what I might paint here could be respected.

IRENE. You can't go now. *(Paces to the liquor table, distraught.)*

ROOSTER. *(Strong.)* I can't think of anything but this artist's colony. It got in my head and everything else got out. To have days to myself and waste them painting my way.

IRENE. *(Loving.)* I'll set up a place in the yard or rent a spot in the park.

41

ROOSTER. If I keep moving, my health will come back.

IRENE. *(With mounting terror.)* Your immune system is shot.

ROOSTER. True... but in North Carolina I'll be supported to work on whatever plane I like.

IRENE. Who knows what will happen if you're not properly cared for?

ROOSTER. Some days I've more energy than others, and when I don't I nap.

IRENE. That's what you should do. Read. Relax.

ROOSTER. But staying here, there's another kind of pain. When I was a boy, I was flattered you wanted my opinion. But now I feel trapped. I can't be on the phone five minutes you don't scream, "Who's that?" If I compliment Monica or any other woman, you grumble. Look...

IRENE. What a horrible—

ROOSTER. I'm not blaming you. I love rich places. Antoine's, Galatoire's.

IRENE. You're irritable because... you're not well...

ROOSTER. I need to be out on my own, meet other artists, see and move–

IRENE. *(Scared, broken.)* You can't go anywhere 'til you're well.

ROOSTER. I don't need your permission. You're jealous, and it's getting worse. I don't know if you can stop it. Until Dad died you never tolerated girls around me.

42

IRENE. Wha'd you talking about?

ROOSTER. In Puerto Vallarta, when I finally had a girl and a commission, you created that awful scene before the people from the Guggenheim....

IRENE. Lies. The Guggenheim threw you into that breakdown.

ROOSTER. But even that pain wasn't enough to make me rebel. I've been thinking a lot about you and Dad lately. I wake up and feel him in the room.

IRENE. Don't talk about your father.

ROOSTER. Ma, I'll come back home. I'm not going forever. I'm your son.

IRENE. How can you tell?

ROOSTER. I've got Louisiana on my driver's license and my birth certificate is recorded here.

IRENE. *(Breaking down.)* This isn't the best time for me. My favorite dog died this morning.

ROOSTER. Which dog?

IRENE. The new Catahoula hound with one crystal eye and a white cross on her forehead. I called her Desdemona.

MONICA. *(Returning)* I heard what happened with your dog.

IRENE. I'm not talking to you. I'm talking to Roo. *(Sobbing.)* My old dog, Ophelia's, in mourning. I hope she doesn't drown herself by the willow tree.

43

(BUNKY enters, pursued by OOZIE. ROOSTER shows them an envelope.)

BUNKY. Somebody died?

ROOSTER. *(Shattered.)* Close. I won an art competition. A residency . On an estate for artists. They give you a cottage and a studio for work.

IRENE. If Roo starts obsessing on painting again, it'll be a catastrophe.

BUNKY. *(Turns on the stereo)* Let's do a happy dance. (**ROOSTER** *nods no.)* You dance the success of this person. The first rule is, "Never dance alone!" *(To* **IRENE**)

IRENE. *(Still crying.)* Dancing's not my preferred activity today.

BUNKY. In Africa they say if you can walk you can sing, and if you can sing, you can dance. *(He and* **IRENE** *dance.)*

(IRENE draws away, snivelling. OOZIE taking BUNKY's hand, and they begin dancing. OOZIE spins by herself in delight. ROOSTER and MONICA observe. BUNKY swipes IRENE's old-fashioned while she isn't looking.)

BUNKY. There's no melody. It's all rhythm, memory, and soul. The fife and drum connect you with being.

IRENE. My son wants to live in a Boy Scout cabin. North Carolina's bursting with nuclear waste. Before you eat their wild duck, you've got to get it tested for radioactivity.

OOZIE. Can you sell paintings there?

IRENE. I wouldn't go any place where you bring your own toilet paper.

OOZIE. Not another Puerta Vallarta.

ROOSTER. I'm going.

IRENE. You can't govern Roo. He was born stubborn, remained stubborn, and will die stubborn, and in the process he'll bury a lot of us with him.

(SOUND: Music stops.)

(ALL sit. ROOSTER gets the painting.)

MONICA. Mrs. Dubonnet, this award's a great honor.

IRENE. How many artists applied, two?

ROOSTER. Here's the painting that won.

IRENE. *(Belligerent.)* I'm embarrassed that this is the best you can do. *(Rings bell)* Where's Angela? I'm tired. **OOZIE** and I made mint jelly all morning. Nobody needs paintings or sculpture. Even the Statue of Liberty is not maintained.

(SOUND: A phone rings offstage.)

(BUNKY exits.)

MONICA. Roo's artwork was judged by an impartial panel.

IRENE. Who're soliciting my donation. The Hyde Museum's not my favorite charity. *(Reaches for her old-fashioned, but her glass is empty.)* Who's stealing my old-fashioneds? *(To* **ROOSTER***)* I'd like to prop your career up, but it'd mean a misallocation of funds. Sometime, I'll outline for you how the family foundation works.

ROOSTER. Don't spoil this.

MONICA. Your mom will be fine once she sees what this means—

IRENE. *(To* **ROOSTER***)* Travel later in life or you'll get bored with it. *(Rises to leave)* I've got to have eye surgery. I can't see a dang thing.

OOZIE. Her eyes come and go. *(Hands her a cane.)*

IRENE. I can walk alone—

OOZIE. If she goes slowly.

(IRENE slightly falls)

MONICA. Mrs. Dubonnet?

IRENE. *(Shakes her head.)* Don't let that woman touch me!

*(**OOZIE** and **ROOSTER** get **IRENE** up but she is very weak and has to lean against them.)*

ROOSTER. Lean on me.

IRENE. Someone's going to slip and sue me for a million dollars.

*(**IRENE** rests her head on **ROOSTER** and walks slowly out supported by **OOZIE**. **MONICA** watches them. **BUNKY** enters, chugging whiskey.)*

BUNKY. Everybody's gone? Lucky me.

MONICA. *(Keeping her voice low)* Wha'd you want?

BUNKY. One kiss. I'm so drunk I got mixed up and hollered for you in the bathroom. Men are weak, sweetheart. What can I do? And women tempt us, you know...

46

MONICA. No closer.

BUNKY. You don't have to love me. It can be worth your while... *(Takes a few steps closer.)* One sweet dance... with a brother's hand...

MONICA. Go.

BUNKY. Bet you'd like to play with me. I like you. You know it. Women know it.

MONICA. No.

BUNKY. Don't be afraid.

MONICA. Stop.

BUNKY. But we have to taste each other first, and we can have a whole meal.

MONICA. Oh God. Move.

BUNKY. Kiss me. It won't kill you.

MONICA. No!

*(Leans head back . . . **MONICA** hits **BUNKY**. He storms about as if he'll beat her.)*

BUNKY. Most girls like it.

END OF SCENE 1

Scene 2

(A week later. 6:00 p.m. Dusk. It's drizzling. **OOZIE** *enters in her Victorian bridal gown, carrying a pearl rosary.* **ROOSTER** *enters in slacks and a gray turtleneck, takes out his camera. He begins to photograph her, moving about easily with the camera.)*

ROOSTER. *(Sets down camera and moves inside the picture)* I'm getting in the frame.

OOZIE. She's so upset about you, she wants to put off my wedding. The heart doctor's doubling her pills! God knows what'll happen if you move to North Carolina...

ROOSTER. She's too rich for the doctors to let her die.

OOZIE. *(To* **ROOSTER***)* Purvis's no comfort. *(Flabbergasted)* He'll postpone our wedding indefinitely to have it on her tab at the Country Club.

ROOSTER. He's an alcoholic.

OOZIE. Purvis's not an alcoholic. He just likes to drink.

ROOSTER. Purvis is eighty-one, but his liver is a hundred and seven.

OOZIE. He's going ahead with this ceremony if I've to drug his oatmeal to do so.

ROOSTER. Whoa.

OOZIE. Stay with Irene till after my wedding. All my life I've dreamed of marriage, but no one offered me safety as a wife and mother. I accepted the gifts of married men and kept my demands small. After Pete died, I stayed with your mother— Maybe she didn't know about...

*(*IRENE *arrives in Victorian wedding attire and on a cane.)*

IRENE. Angela just sits in the kitchen, and when I ask her what's wrong, she cries. *(Pause)* I've three maids, but no dinner.

ROOSTER. Everybody smile. *(Takes a photo.)*

IRENE. I'm one breath short of the grave. Roo'll put me in Metairie Cemetery next week! I don't take it personal. If you take it personal, it's four old-fashioneds in the room at night.

(BUNKY enters. He wears several thick ropes of Mardi Gras beads over Victorian attire. He does a jig over to the liquor cart.)

(SOUND: A parade passing.)

BUNKY. Bacchus parade's passing. I caught some beads with gold babies.

ROOSTER. Liquor's one way to offset a glum outlook.

BUNKY. I love Mardi Gras. These lavish stupidities.

ROOSTER. Everybody line up.

(ROOSTER shoots various poses during the following sequence. Parade passes with fanfare.)

IRENE. *(To BUNKY)* Stand by me. Grandpa loved Carnival. Three times he was king of a parade and ball. For me Carnival's the divine element in New Orleans. It's the part that connects us with history.

OOZIE. Ah, yes. Dancing at those balls with men in silver boots—

IRENE. Sitting in the roped-off section for wives. Mardi Gras.

ROOSTER. Everybody smile. Say, "Carnival."

ALL. Carnival.

IRENE. In the old days, Bunky, there were mule-drawn floats and flambeaux carriers tap-dancing for quarters.

BUNKY. Look at that monstrous float!

IRENE. Let's go on the balcony and get a better look.

(IRENE exits with OOZIE. BUNKY waits. He empties the glass, takes a second.)

ROOSTER. Angela's...

BUNKY. *(Broken.)* Just back from Oschner Clinic. She's lost a lot of blood...

ROOSTER. And the baby?

BUNKY. *(Distraught.)* I'm not a father... Don't look like that.

ROOSTER. You should grow up. What are you, twenty-one, twenty-two? What do you want from me?

BUNKY. *(Desperate, still in love.)* Angela is crying, and I can't stop her. I sat through her sob story, even though I was vaguely destroyed by it. I need to give her something.

ROOSTER. Maybe Monica can help.

BUNKY. I can't ask her. I wanted to... but I... I made a fool of myself.

ROOSTER. Wha'd you do?

BUNKY. I wanted to kiss her, I think.

ROOSTER. What? Did you hurt her?

BUNKY. The whole thing happened too quickly...

ROOSTER. You embarrassed her? You're drinking more and more? You act like a zombie. A couple of years and you'll be an alcoholic.

BUNKY. *(Closes eyes as if to nap.)* I've given up thinking. Swear to God.

ROOSTER. Go to Angela. Support her. *(Writes him a check.)*

BUNKY. After the parade. How bleak it is here. Darkness and rain and funeral gloom. Day after day throughout Carnival. Never a flash of sun. How I loved the parades. I'd follow them halfway to Canal Street. Move in step to the hard-charging sounds. Ground moving beneath my feet. And the showers of trinkets from the floats. You see these floats, soft big puffs moving down the street. Hearing the sirens, and the rush of jazz. Watching the gypsies come in and out and the Indians. Just yesterday I was a school boy. Everything was so easy... so... Football games, homecoming and sweet-sixteen parties. Convertibles and girls and...

*(*BUNKY *falls asleep.* IRENE *enters with* OOZIE*.)*

IRENE. Angela's crying. Miss Falcon's somewhere watching the parades. *(To* ROOSTER*)* I want to compliment you on that woman. She could con the whole family sequentially.

OOZIE. Whenever I see her, her hem's wrong. Doesn't she know the length this year?

IRENE. Faded smocks. Hair in a desperate condition...

ROOSTER. She's filled me with profound hope.

IRENE. Cohabitate if you must, in one of those rabbit hutches in the dark parts of town. Wear Birkenstock sandals and look painfully thin. I can float above it. Soon all you'll have is the memory of money.

OOZIE. Calm down, honey. What you need is a drink.

IRENE. *(To* **ROOSTER***)* Don't expect me to support you both. I'd have to be really desperate or really... Dead!

OOZIE. *(Handing her a drink)* You'll feel better with a toddy.

IRENE. I called that cabin place. They don't have plumbing or electricity. I'll have to speak to Monica.

ROOSTER. Don't you dare.

IRENE. Dare what?

ROOSTER. Talk to her, go near her, accuse her.

IRENE. I'm trying to maintain a veneer of civilization. To smooth over something rough with—something refined.

ROOSTER. No, you're not.

IRENE. *(Panicky.)* I've spent time checking up on this flea-bitten cabin place.

ROOSTER. Who asked you? I said keep out.

IRENE. You just want to go there to drink and screw this girl.

ROOSTER. You're going too far.

IRENE. You'll sing a different tune... when you relapse.

ROOSTER. For God's sake I... what... what's gotten into you?

IRENE. Don't... come near me.

53

ROOSTER. Tell me. Why do you want to hurt me?

IRENE. *(Quiet)* What's the point of running off?

(IRENE walks over and strokes his hair.)

ROOSTER. Oh, Ma. I yearn to travel... to fall in love with life over and over again. *(Pause)* Ma, you and I both know there's a difference between removing death and extending life. I'd like to postpone dying as long as possible.

IRENE. *(Terrified.)* Do not use the D word.

ROOSTER. Everything changes in the shadow of...

IRENE. You don't know what you are talking about.

ROOSTER. There's a special light that comes from a different state of being. It's almost blue-white. Colors I've seen in Florence and Rome around the cathedrals at night. You lose your edge. You merge with everything. And yet, you see sharper. The sun, the rain, you smell the grass when you go out in the garden. You can almost taste the Resurrection ferns... the green leafy plant on trees. Light and color intensify. The purity at dawn, the stark reality at noon, and the romantic red of sunset, the final burst of color before blackness. Then there's twilight, the hour of gentleness, so mysterious, so sad. Nothing moved; then it turned dark. Time's going by so fast, it makes me mad.... I want to go to North Carolina.

IRENE. Take my advice; say, "No." *(Pause)* You haven't real choices. . .

ROOSTER. What do you mean?

IRENE. You're going to have a relapse. It's as simple as that.

ROOSTER. Why don't you let me find out?

IRENE. *(Scared.)* I know how necessary it is for you to be quiet.

ROOSTER. I don't want to rot.

IRENE. You wouldn't. You haven't listened to me since she got here.

ROOSTER. *(Directly to his mother.)* Do you think this decision's nothing for me? I've been practicing how to talk to you. I look around the room, this nowhere space where I dream. I turn on the lights and tell myself not to feel, to think, that you'll want what's best for me. I look at the ornaments, the photographs, the relics of my youth. Books, paints, papers. Everywhere I look I find a feeling. Each object recalls a scene. When I gaze about, I'm a boy with idle dreams. I've stared through the memories. Opened the sealed doors of grief. Said good-bye to all the fantasies and let them evaporate like so much smoke. *(Pause)* I'm going to ask Monica to live with me.

IRENE. Oh, God.

ROOSTER. I'm asking her tonight.

IRENE. *(Horrified.)* A man in your state can't marry.

ROOSTER. I'm almost out of my mind. Can't you see that?

IRENE. I can't believe you're doing this.

ROOSTER. I'm going to keep asking her till she says "yes." When I was a little boy, I decided that I was no good. I ran to this room, when I heard you and Dad fighting. I decided it was my fault. You rushed in here and I couldn't get you out, not even when I, oh God, pushed you and screamed, "Go on. Go on." So I slept in the chair and let you stay. I know you depend on me for someone to be close with. To do things for. You're important to me. Ma, needing to please you doesn't fade with age.

IRENE. I've got... to tell you... since you won't let me protect you—

ROOSTER. Yes...?

IRENE. All this business about being exhausted... being unable to paint... all this isn't... the real problem. . .

ROOSTER. What?

IRENE. The sickness you've contracted... can't be cured. The doctors told me.

ROOSTER. That's not true—

IRENE. Your body's... breaking down.

ROOSTER. You mustn't... say things like that.

IRENE. I don't... I don't want to. But it's a fact. You haven't got long.

ROOSTER. Nothing's hopeless.

IRENE. You've already had one setback.

ROOSTER. Before Monica arrived. It went away.

IRENE. It could happen again... soon, at any time. I want you to stay home... near me, the doctors...

ROOSTER. That's what I can't take. Lying here... till I become helpless. Monica!

IRENE. You can't count on her. She'll be off soon as she meets a richer artist with bigger rooms. I know these semi-pious types, feeding you illusions while they soak up your money. I wonder who she'll find to mooch off in North Carolina. She's an imposter.

ROOSTER. You've said that once too often. Liar.

IRENE. I told Doctor Ryan that you and your fly-by-night nurse might run off. If you don't quiet down, you will be hauled off to the hospital and she will be reported to the A.M.A. and lose her license. You get what I'm saying.

ROOSTER. Out, out, out. Out, out, out!!

IRENE. Oozie! Oozie! Where did I put my drink?

(IRENE stumbles out.)

(ROOSTER collapses on the day bed and dims the lights.)

ROOSTER. You're a bully. You're always... in somebody's face. *(Moments later, MONICA enters, covered in strands of beads and in street attire.)*

(SOUND: The Bacchus parade rumbles in the distance through a screaming crowd.)

MONICA. They're throwing doubloons by the handful. Showers of gold. This is the city where trees wear pearls. *(Turns up the lights)* Look, I've got six purple beads and green ones with gold babies.

ROOSTER. No. Damn it. Turn the light out.

MONICA. Why have it so dark?

ROOSTER. Because I've been accused of being a sucker, of lying to myself.

57

(She quietly opens her satchel and takes his pulse)

MONICA. You're not turning down the award?

ROOSTER. *(Rips the device off his arm.)* I didn't say that.

MONICA. I take back the question with apologies. *(Hands him pills and water)* You don't want to worm your way through it?

ROOSTER. Something like that. Mom's a study in cement, like she's mired in gray. After an hour with her I'm racked out.

MONICA. When you're away a while, you'll love her again and miss the place.

(On the street there is a general hubbub, people yelling, the roar of a motor car.)

ROOSTER. There go the gypsies! Hah. Hah. The last of the gypsies. *(Tries to laugh again)* I'll throw them some beads. Hey y'all. Want to come up? Hey there. Throw me something.

MONICA. You're working yourself up doing that.

ROOSTER. The last of the gypsies.

MONICA. Stop it.

ROOSTER. Give me those beads. *(Grabs at her beads)*

MONICA. You're cutting me doing that.

ROOSTER. Hurry.

MONICA. Let me do it.

ROOSTER. Take them off.

MONICA. No, no, they won't come off. Wait.

ROOSTER. I'll have to break them off you.

MONICA. Wait.

ROOSTER. Too late, they're gone. *(Heads for the door. She blocks him.)* Out my way.

MONICA. Where're you going?

ROOSTER. To find the gypsies.

MONICA. Not tonight.

(He starts for the door)

ROOSTER. Out my way.

(He trips, rushes back to the bed, throws himself down.)

ROOSTER. I'd like a knock-out injection. Monica?

MONICA. Yes?

ROOSTER. What're you doing?

MONICA. Watching you.

ROOSTER. How long do you plan to do that?

MONICA. Long as it takes. Can I do something for you?

ROOSTER. Let me go out.

MONICA. Not in such a crowd.

ROOSTER. I can't stand being pent up.

MONICA. You'll have to take it awhile.

ROOSTER. A man can go crazy with the jitters.

MONICA. You can't keep carrying your mother's pain.

ROOSTER. Psychoanalysis is out.

MONICA. I thought it was just coming into fashion in the South.

ROOSTER. Soon. Be patient. Some people drink. Some take a pill. Others— You know Ma keeps a loaded gun by her bed. I never go in this house without screaming her name, because I'm afraid she might accidentally shoot me. Now I'm afraid of much worse.

MONICA. She's a survivor. She can take care of herself.

ROOSTER. "To take care of someone" has a double meaning.

MONICA. How long can you keep losing chances? Little bits of life. Shreds of dreams. God wants success for you, but you must give something up? You can't hold God in one hand and family in the other.

ROOSTER. I've been juggling for—

MONICA. Set yourself free.

ROOSTER. Dogs have been known to go crazy when their leash was cut. What if my body gives out, and I can't do the things you want?

MONICA. Pray for grace. God will help you.

ROOSTER. Could He?

MONICA. Why not?

ROOSTER. You think God can help me all the time?

MONICA. Every second.

(He kisses her violently, desperately. She draws away.)

ROOSTER. I like your hair. There're so many things I take delight in. You mostly. Nice to be young. To see trees like lace against the sky. You've gorgeous eyes. Forest green. One day, I'm going to take you to Antoine's. Buy you whatever you want. As long as you wear green. Green for spring time. Green for Christmas. It's the kind of bartering a husband can do. *(Pause)* Marry me.

(IRENE enters and glares at ROOSTER.)

IRENE. Rooster!

ROOSTER. Please get out.

IRENE. Monica, I need you to help with supper.

MONICA. Sure.

IRENE. What're you doing?

MONICA. Bringing in the plates.

IRENE. Oozie will do that. You mustn't think I condemn all travel. I imagine there're some invalids who can improve temporarily. Most Southerners would rather live with security than wait for a dream to take fire. Sit... here. I'd like a word with you. Why do you keep pushing my son?

61

MONICA. He's improving.

IRENE. Hardly. Roo feels safe in New Orleans; it's the opposite of the fractured feeling he gets back east—

MONICA. Every day he's stronger. He'll do even better in the mountains.

IRENE. North Carolina?

MONICA. I've been researching his condition. In the mountains...

IRENE. I'm not going to rescue him like we did in Ensenada when he fled to the beach. Called the seagulls our ancestors. Painted from can't see to can't see. Driven by some undisguised lamentation.

MONICA. He wants your blessing to go.

IRENE. Ah, North Carolina. And after that, what is next?

MONICA. Don't mock him.

IRENE. I'm not. I lived with the boy all his life. He's mine to use. But this time I... I can't teaspoon him back to life. *(Pause)* What are you?

MONICA. His nurse.

IRENE. Is that all you are?

MONICA. That's enough.

IRENE. You're certainly very sure of yourself, but I'm not convinced you've any education at all. Where are your degrees? You come here and set yourself up as some radical healer. You've no friends, no phone calls. You never go out with any normal men.

MONICA. I know you lost your husband. I lost mine too.

IRENE. No, the problem is my son.

MONICA. You mean his fragile state and his...

IRENE. You're not for him and he's not for you. My intuition is like radar. *(Pause)* How long were you at it before you knew you were on your way... with my relentlessly lovable son? A week? Using your eyes as a sexual organ and this hocus-pocus spirituality as a guise.

MONICA. I'm not that kind of person.

IRENE. You wouldn't be the first girl thrown from nursing—for hysterical excess.

MONICA. Oh, no... no, Mrs. Dubonnet.

IRENE. It's important to have a fairly fast start in medicine, and my comments could destroy you.

MONICA. You wouldn't do that... you couldn't... I'm just trying to help... to heal.

IRENE. Some spook is what you are.

MONICA. Roo needs to use his days well.

IRENE. Painting made him sick. And your nasty affair will make him worse. Go pack. You're fired.

MONICA. Don't give me commands.

IRENE. You do what I tell you to do, or I'll have you removed.

MONICA. You wouldn't.

IRENE. Dragging a sick boy to the countryside for his money. *(Removes and raises her gun)*

MONICA. God almighty.

IRENE. Tomorrow morning. Huck will drive you to the airport and buy you a ticket to—

MONICA. Wait... we've got to talk.

IRENE. I'm telling you. Get out. *(Calls)* Oozie Come here. Oozie.

(OOZIE hurries in with food)

IRENE. Oozie, Miss Falcon is leaving.

OOZIE. With Roo?

IRENE. Huck will take out all the paintings. The garbage man will pick them up. I paid for them, and they belong to me.

MONICA. I promised to take care of them. Each painting a little piece of his heart.

IRENE. All graphics and no content.

MONICA. I won't let you do this.

OOZIE. An old-fashioned?

IRENE. Get out.

MONICA. I'm not leaving.

(IRENE shoots. BUNKY comes in.)

BUNKY. *(Rushing up)* Put down the gun.

OOZIE. Get back.

(They struggle. **IRENE** *shoots wildly at the ceiling.* **OOZIE** *collapses.)*

OOZIE. She hit me. My arm. My leg! No, my shoulder. It's inside me, burning. Burning inside of my dress.

BUNKY. For God's sake. She's still breathing.

IRENE. She can't die. She's getting married next week.

END OF SCENE 2

Scene 3

(One week later. Five p.m., **OOZIE**'s *wedding day. Light rain.*
IRENE *crosses the stage slowly on* **BUNKY'S** *arm. Both are
dressed in Victorian wedding attire as in the previous scene but they
also wear coats and gloves.)*

IRENE. *(Yells.)* Huck, take down the guns and lock the gates. *(To*
BUNKY*)* Thanks for walking me, precious.

BUNKY. *(Takes a silver bell from his pocket)* Want a wedding
bell?

IRENE. When I looked at Oozie decked out in that going away
suit, my feet almost gave way. She looked happy.

BUNKY. Thank God she took off that sling.

IRENE. *(Pauses to catch her breath)* Wait. Let me dry your face;
you're damp, sugar.

BUNKY. Drizzle.

(She dries his face affectionately with her handkerchief.)

IRENE. I'm changing my will. Roo's hurt me so. Refusing to be in
the wedding party. Arriving with that woman.

(They exit. **ROOSTER** *enters. He wears a jacket over slacks from
the previous scene. He looks weaker and drained.* **ROOSTER** *calls
to his mother.)*

ROOSTER. Ma. I wanted to say good-bye. Hey, Ma? I'm still your
son.

IRENE. *(Returning to the doorway with* **BUNKY***)* I haven't a son
anymore. Who's this stranger? *(Exits.)*

BUNKY. *(Calls back before exiting)* Try her after her nap.

ROOSTER. *(To* **BUNKY***)* Right.

*(***MONICA** *enters in a lovely dress, accented in green. Some combination from the previous scene's attire is possible.* **ROOSTER** *glances at the garden.)*

ROOSTER. The sun's already fading through the oak trees.

MONICA. *(Looks at her watch)* You've three hours before the plane.

ROOSTER. Yes.

MONICA. The next hour's mine.

ROOSTER. All of it?

MONICA. Every minute.

ROOSTER. I've never been this tired in all my life. Never.

MONICA. Come. Sit. *(Hands him some water.)* Rest. Shut your eyes a minute.

ROOSTER. I see more when I close my eyes.

MONICA. You do?

ROOSTER. If I shut my eyes, I see you.

MONICA. What about me?

ROOSTER. It's... it's...

MONICA. What?

(Rooster takes **MONICA**'s *hand, sits her beside him.)*

ROOSTER. I plotted out our relationship, and I thought it was going to be real sexy. Every time I came near, you looked embarrassed, off to the side, and then you left.

MONICA. I didn't want to ruin anything between us.

ROOSTER. I felt ashamed because I'd wake up in these hot sweats and you acted like a nun. I'd such sexy ideas in such an utterly nonsexy place.

MONICA. Did you—well.

ROOSTER. You knew it. Huh?

MONICA. Every morning when I saw myself in your eyes, it reminded me I wasn't buried with my husband.

ROOSTER. You never told me?

MONICA. You kept me going.

ROOSTER. I want to remember this place... in case I don't see it again. My father sat right here with the evening paper. He didn't read the obituaries. Most of his friends were dead by fifty-five. At night he came to this room and drank. Southerners mark rooms by events, not years. This is the room where my father died. Dad was an alcoholic, but he'd a cat called Christmas. Its ears had been burnt in a fire. Every night that cat waited for Dad at the garage. And he'd walk it under his umbrella to this room. When Dad died, Christmas got in here and tore the room apart. Wadded the drapes. Knocked everything on the floor. Howled. Tonight, I feel like Christmas.

MONICA. The last year with my husband was a battle I lost every day and started the next. My husband wanted to die. He couldn't stand getting weak. He was strong before. Raced motorcycles for the thrill. He didn't want anyone to see that he couldn't walk, so I'd help him down to his motorcycle, and he'd drive it to the mailbox. The bike roaring beneath his thin legs. He'd come back to the stairs, exhausted and sit. And when no one was looking, he'd ease himself up one step at a time. I smiled from the window—so attentive to what he was doing, merged with his courage. But finally the world of matter faded away, and he gave up, and I gave up. It's started to rain again.

ROOSTER. New Orleans is saying good-bye.

MONICA. She's crying because she loves you so.

ROOSTER. *(Pause)* I asked you to marry me, and you never responded.

MONICA. You'll soon be working nonstop, free of the concerns that worried you.

ROOSTER. Look, I won't be here tomorrow. Have you forgotten? I won't be here tomorrow.

MONICA. Yes, I'd forgotten. It actually slipped my mind for a moment.

ROOSTER. You like rings?

MONICA. What are you doing?

ROOSTER. I'm putting one on your finger.

MONICA. It's a fine diamond. Someday, somebody will be happy with it.

ROOSTER. Fight again. I'll be on your side. I'm going to live. Come with me. *(He kisses her.)*

MONICA. *(The rain begins to pour again.)* The best rain doesn't have warning. It is merciful. *(They exit together.)*

END OF PLAY
APPENDIX

(Note: New cast has MEMBERS OF THE CARNIVAL COURT: 7 women, 1 man; Total cast 10 women, 3 men.)

(To Replace Act II, scene 1).

ACT II

Scene 1

(The day room. Three weeks later. Six p.m. The afternoon is drawing to a close. Somethign like Wagner's Lohengrin's Bridal Chorus plays on the stereo. A lighted lamp stands on the table. IRENE, in a Victorian "mother-of-the bride's" dress, is sitting reading a "Town and Country" magazine. OOZIE is dressed in Victorian wedding attire complete with tiara and veil. She stands at the back of the room for a moment with her hands clasping a nosegay. Then she comes back near the table, picks up a mirror and looks at her face.)

OOZIE. *(Imperious)* How do you like my dress?

IRENE. Pretty, but it's not soft enough for me. We've different tastes.

OOZIE. That's what I wanted. Purvis accepts me at face value. I don't want to look frail like I'm living in a fairy tale.

IRENE. You don't.

OOZIE. I just hate the way I look. I had my hair done. I liked it for about an hour.

IRENE. *(Looks at **OOZIE***'s hair)* Strange shade. Looks like chicken feathers.

OOZIE. It's my natural color so my hair's a restoration. Now I've passed the big four-oh I've switched from cheap barettes to a headband. And a Wonder bra..

IRENE. Big fifty, and you're pushed up too high!

OOZIE. Why are you nasty with me? Roo's the one you should yell at. *(Striding up and down the stage)* He's with that nurse. And what's more, she's not from here. She's an import.

IRENE. To think Roo was in "Life Magazine" at twenty as one of the red hot one hundred.

OOZIE. It's not just the photo but who takes it.

IRENE. But if your photo's not to the paper on time...

OOZIE. I will not get the upper right-hand corner of the Living Section. I know. I don't know if I'm frustrated or disappointed.

IRENE. You always have problems with distinctions. Frustrated is like an itch. Disappointed is like a tear.

OOZIE. *(Puts **IRENE***'s hand to her chest.)* Roo's giving me high blood pressure. Can you feel that...Ba-bump, ba-bump. Hear that?

71

IRENE. No. I smell my perfume.

OOZIE: Roo doesn't call home, if he doesn't feel like it. He doesn't know they've invented South Central Bell?

IRENE. Never do anything for men thinking you're going to get what you want. To be effective, one needs to expect catastrophe. This should be easy. I've watched so many boys in the Garden District acquire an unfeeling attitude. They stay at home but they aren't there except when they're tired, hungry, or broke. For entertainment, they torment their relatives. Women are by nature more sensitive than men. We've to curb ourselves to keep them. It's not their fault we're more intelligent. We provide amusement. We have for centuries.

(SOUND: The clock chimes.)

OOZIE. Fitting end to a lousy day. I'm going to get changed and drive myself somewhere nice. *(Starts to go, stops, and crosses to the phone, dials.)* Lord! I've no car. Purvis promised to lend me his.

IRENE. You drive a car until it smokes, and he won't let you do that to a Jaguar...

OOZIE. I hope his secretary's not using it.

IRENE. Already? These questionable generosities.

(IRENE returns to her "Town and Country," looking preoccupied. Awkward silence. OOZIE sits, yanks off her shoes, and sticks her feet out. Horrified.)

OOZIE. My feet hurt. I need a toe reduction. I just hate my toes. My second one's too long. *(Looks for ROOSTER. Holds up her ring)* This is a two-carat diamond. It's very nice, but Purvis gave his first wife a five-carat flawless one from Tiffany's! She kept it after the divorce.

IRENE. You can keep yours, too.

OOZIE. *(Crosses and brings* **IRENE** *her drink.)* I'm not marrying Purvis unless I get jewelry of equal value. Purvis is not my dream man because he lies, steals, and cheats.

IRENE. Every man should have on his desk, "The truth stops here."

OOZIE. If only he would lie to other people and tell me the truth.

IRENE. They lie once, twice. Then lying becomes addictive.

OOZIE. *(Stuffs Kleenex in her armpits.)* I'm sweating like a pig!

IRENE. Ladies "moisten." They don't sweat!

OOZIE. Keeping myself intact is impossible. I've got to move in sections and reassemble once it's safe.

IRENE. I'd say things are fine, but they're not. Just like that summer you and Pete were in this house.

OOZIE. *(Clears her throat.)* You and Pete weren't talking except at the Carnival balls.

IRENE. You don't have to chat to be valued.

OOZIE. Pete was so easy, so good, so...

IRENE. Try not to talk so much, so we can live with each other.

*(*BUNKY *enters impatiently, hurries over to the liquor cart. HE pours a fistful of aspirins and unscrews a bottle, and ignores Irene.)*

IRENE. Another bird in flight. *(To* **BUNKY***)* You didn't tell me, "Hello!"

BUNKY. I said "Hello" this morning when I saw you in the parlor.

IRENE. But is one hello a day enough?

OOZIE. He can't talk to us mortals.

IRENE. You get up looking for a drink?

BUNKY. I'm trying to kill this headache.

OOZIE. By mixing alcohol and aspirin!

BUNKY. I drink more when it rains. You, see, there's reality, and there's real reality, under everything else. If you get too much into real reality, you'll drink too. Salut.

(He pours himself bourbon and a glass of water.)

IRENE. I've nearly been ignored to death on some occasions.

(The phone rings. **BUNKY** *hurries back in.* **OOZIE** *grabs the phone.)*

OOZIE. *(Into phone)* Hello... Who? What? *(To* **BUNKY***)* Ocshner Clinic. *(To* **BUNKY***)* They hung up.

BUNKY. *(Terrified for Angela.)* I'm going to sit in the rain. I'm talked out.

OOZIE. Wait. Didn't I see you there? I was in a class, "Intimacy for Seniors."

BUNKY. I wasn't there.

OOZIE. Well, it must have a been a holograph of you!

(*SOUND:* A phone rings. **BUNKY** *grasps it and whispers into the phone.*)

BUNKY. *(Desperately.)* Hello. It's sure? Yes... yes...

(**BUNKY** *slips offstage with the phone.* **IRENE** *peers at the garden.*)

OOZIE. Finally the king arrives. I can't wait to give him my own hospitality.

(**ROOSTER** *and* **MONICA** *enter the garden whispering.*)

ROOSTER. Audubon's the most sensual park. Geese gliding in the ponds.

MONICA. Camellias. So big and light.

(**ROOSTER** *and* **MONICA** *enter through the garden door.*)

ROOSTER. Every time I go out I feel I can paint again. I'm a magnet for the color.

IRENE. *(Truly worried.)* You want to get worse? *(Points to the door)* You're throwing the cooling system off whack.

ROOSTER. I cancelled our sitting.

IRENE. How could you? She's afraid she's losing her looks, and there wasn't much to begin with.

OOZIE. Only someone heartless could fail to see how important a good photo is to a woman... nearly forty.

IRENE. *(Rises irritably.)* Fifty. Can you help the girl?

MONICA. *(Exiting)* It's Roo's choice, isn't it?

OOZIE. *(To* **ROOSTER***)* I need a great wedding picture. I've had two premarital divorces.

IRENE. Don't cry and ruin your mascara. Just because you've been under the knife doesn't mean you're photogenic. *(Exiting)*

OOZIE. Yes, well... Your mother is a witch. Still, it's hard to leave. The big wonderful bedrooms. The polished Cadillac by the door.

ROOSTER. *(Angry at her.)* It was a good place to live from zero to eight.

OOZIE. We'd sit in the dining room, jingling our glasses, popping a pecan.

ROOSTER. I don't want to talk about the way it was.

OOZIE. OK. Good-bye, Saint Charles Avenue. Good-bye to the grand piano. And the garden. And cut-glass front doors... satin comforters sliding off your legs. Does anyone value New Orleans while they're living in it?

ROOSTER. *(Seething.)* Dad did maybe, he did some.

OOZIE: Sometimes I don't know if I was happy or miserable in this house.

ROOSTER. It could have been nice to live here... if we didn't have this cloud of uncertainty. When you and Dad were on the porch with that little light on, I'd go to the gallery and watch the streetcars clang by. And in her room Ma would sit up late, immobilized, the help grumbling in the kitchen. Dad and you. Just talk or fire. *(Pause)* I realize I was born as a last attempt to save their marriage.

OOZIE. I wished you were mine.

ROOSTER. *(Points outside.)* Look, the rain's cooled it off. Ma's looking for the parade. I look like her. I never realized before how overwhelming she is... so much love and yet somehow a lie inside all the affection.

OOZIE. I never loved any other man. Can't you forgive me?

ROOSTER. Sometimes I think if my mother had the right loving, she'd be warmer... Parade's coming!

OOZIE. Soon I'll be your aunt of, with, by, and from the state of Texas.

(IRENE enters to police sirens)

(OOZIE exits)

IRENE. Oozie? What's wrong? Roo. Have you been tormenting Oozie?

ROOSTER. *(Suddenly confident.)* I wanted you to be the first to know. I'm right next to a change, but not yet in it. *(Struggles with himself)* Yesterday and again today, I told myself it's impossible... Sit. Please. You ever notice how colors change and certain shapes are lit up? *(Brass band passes)* I feel hope.

IRENE. Hope has been unfashionable for a long time.

ROOSTER. I know. When men leave, people see it as heroic, but when...

IRENE. *(Affectionately.)* Be thankful you've a home.

ROOSTER. I thought I'd never concentrate again... not like before. Then the Hyde Museum started hitting me with phone calls— I got a grant. A year's retreat in North Carolina. It's one of those rare miracle days that blow your mind. I'm going to travel again. Paint my signature work. I can't do a miracle here because I'm the son of the son of the son.

(Doorbell rings. Street noise and hubbub.)

IRENE. There they are!! You belong to a family who embodied the best of tradition.

(MUSIC: "If Ever I Cease to Love.")

(Carnival Parade: A **KING** *and* **QUEEN** *and six* **LADIES-IN-WAIING** *enter and parade around the room. They are dressed elaborately in Elizabethan long gowns and courtly garb. The* **KING** *wears a curtain or wax mask and high silk boots. Both he and the* **QUEEN** *wear crowns and wave scepters)*

IRENE. I invited the court from Proteus. We'll need to toast the Queen and watch their grand march.

(The **COURT** *parade around the room)*

IRENE. *(To* **ROOSTER***)* Everyone wants you to be King next year.

OOZIE. *(Rushing in with champagne)* This is such an honor their coming off the float.

BUNKY. *(Darting in with glasses)* They only stop here and at the Mayor's!

IRENE. I added up the years our family has been involved in Carnival, and it came to one hundred twenty-three.

(Acknowledges the **KING** *and* **QUEEN***)*

Your highness. *(To* **ROOSTER***)* Bow.... One day...I hope... you'll dress like a king, in white velvet with a cap and plume. You'll ride

78

horseback before the floats... then escort the queen in the grand march around the ballroom.

(BUNKY brings her a scepter and crown enshrined on a table. She puts it on and the **COURT** *applaud her)*

IRENE. *(To* **ROOSTER***)* The Carnival Ball links the South with European culture. Your great-grandmother, grandmother, and I were queens—

ROOSTER. *(To self)* I am so fed up with this.

IRENE. When you're Queen of Rex, the doors of society swing open.

(Sound: Musicians play something like, "If Ever I Cease to Love." All dance.)

(IRENE brings the **KING** *and* **QUEEN** *more champagne)*

QUEEN. Remember when Roo costumed in Proteus ball—

KING. When he was ten.

LADY-IN-WAITING. As the son of Paul Revere.

LADY-IN-WAITING. Now he must continue his very deep roots to the city.

QUEEN. *(To* **ROOSTER***)* You don't need to separate yourself . . . to paint.

LADY-IN-WAITING. You can come with us. Repaint our Mardi Gras floats.

(Sirens race outside)

ALL REVELERS. *Laissez les bons temps roulez.* Goodbye!

(REVELERS parade out, followed by **OOZIE** *and* **BUNKY***)*

IRENE. *(To* **ROO***)* In time your paintings will disappear, but Mardi Gras and its traditions will survive.

ROOSTER. I don't believe what I might paint here could be respected.

IRENE. You can't go away now. *(Paces to the liquor table, distraught.)*

ROOSTER. *(Strong.)* I can't think of anything but this artist's colony. It got in my head and everything else got out. To have days to myself and waste them painting my way.

IRENE. *(Loving.)* I'll set up a place in the yard or rent a spot in the park.

ROOSTER. If I keep moving, my health will come back.

IRENE. *(With mounting terror.)* Your immune system is shot.

ROOSTER. True... but in North Carolina I'll be supported to work on whatever plane I like.

IRENE. Who knows what will happen if you're not properly cared for?

ROOSTER. Some days I've more energy than others, and when I don't I nap.

IRENE. That's what you should do. Read. Relax.

ROOSTER. But staying here, there's another kind of pain. When I was a boy, I was flattered you wanted my opinion. But now I feel trapped. I can't be on the phone five minutes you don't scream, "Who's that?" If I compliment Monica or any other woman, you grumble. Look...

IRENE. What a horrible—

ROOSTER. I'm not blaming you. I love rich places. Antoine's, Galatoire's.

IRENE. You're irritable because... you're not well...

ROOSTER. I need to be out on my own, meet other artists, see and move—

IRENE. *(Scared, broken.)* You can't go anywhere 'til you're well.

ROOSTER. I don't need your permission. You're jealous, and it's getting worse. I don't know if you can stop it. Until Dad died you never tolerated girls around me.

IRENE. Wha'd you talking about?

ROOSTER. In Puerto Vallarta, when I finally had a girl and a commission, you created that awful scene before the people from the Guggenheim....

IRENE. Lies. The Guggenheim threw you into that breakdown.

ROOSTER. But even that pain wasn't enough to make me rebel. I've been thinking a lot about you and Dad lately. I wake up and feel him in the room.

IRENE. Don't talk about your father.

ROOSTER. Ma, I'll come back home. I'm not going forever. I'm your son.

81

IRENE. How can you tell?

ROOSTER. I've got Louisiana on my driver's license and my birth certificate is recorded here.

IRENE. *(Breaking down.)* This isn't the best time for me. My favorite dog died this morning.

ROOSTER. Which dog?

IRENE. The new Catahoula hound with one crystal eye and a white cross on her forehead. I called her Desdemona.

(MONICA enters from the parade)

MONICA. *(Returning)* I heard what happened with your dog.

IRENE. I'm not talking to you. I'm talking to Roo. *(Sobbing.)* My old dog, Ophelia's, in mourning. I hope she doesn't drown herself by the willow tree.

(BUNKY enters, pursued by OOZIE and two LADIES-IN-WAITING giggling.)

BUNKY. The float's caught on an oak tree. So we thought we'd grab another drink. *(He downs IRENE's old fashioned then pours more champagne for LADIES)* Somebody died?

ROOSTER. *(Shattered.)* Close. I won an art competition. A residency . On an estate for artists. They give you a cottage and a studio for work.

IRENE. If Roo starts obsessing on painting again, it'll be a catastrophe.

BUNKY. *(Hears parade band)* Let's do a happy dance.
(ROOSTER *nods no.)* You dance the success of this person. *(To* **IRENE)**The first rule is, "Never dance alone!"

IRENE. *(Still crying.)* Dancing's not my preferred activity today.

BUNKY. In Africa they say if you can walk you can sing, and if you can sing, you can dance. *(He and* **IRENE** *dance.)*

*(***IRENE** *draws away,* **OOZIE** *takes* **BUNKY**'*s hand, and they begin dancing.* **OOZIE** *spins by herself in delight. The* **LADIES-IN-WAITING** *drink and dance.* **ROOSTER** *and* **MONICA** *observe.* **BUNKY** *swipes a bottle of champagne, gives it to the ladies and they dance upstage.)*

BUNKY. There's no melody. It's all rhythm, memory, and soul. The fife and drum connect you with being.

IRENE. *(To* **OOZIE)** My son wants to live in a Boy Scout cabin. North Carolina's bursting with nuclear waste. Before you eat their wild duck, you've got to get it tested for radioactivity.

OOZIE. Can you sell paintings there?

IRENE. I wouldn't go any place where you bring your own toilet paper.

OOZIE. Not another Puerta Vallarta.

ROOSTER. I'm going.

IRENE. You can't govern Roo. He was born stubborn, remained stubborn, and will die stubborn, and in the process he'll bury a lot of us with him.

*(SOUND: MUSIC stops. Doorbell rings. Sirens go off on street and the **LADIES** and **BUNKY** rush out. **OOZIE** and **IRENE** sit. **MONICA** looks at **ROOSTER** and **IRENE**.)*

MONICA. Mrs. Dubonnet, this award's a great honor.

IRENE. How many artists applied, two?

ROOSTER. Here's the painting that won.

IRENE. *(Belligerent.)* I'm embarrassed that this is the best you can do. *(Rings bell)* Where's Angela? I'm tired. Oozie and I made mint jelly all morning. Nobody needs paintings or sculpture. Even the Statue of Liberty is not maintained.

(SOUND: A parade starts up.)

MONICA. Roo's artwork was judged by an impartial panel.

IRENE. Who're soliciting my donation. The Hyde Museum's not my favorite charity. *(Reaches for her old-fashioned, but her glass is empty.)* Who's stealing my old-fashioneds? *(To **ROOSTER**)* I'd like to prop your career up, but it'd mean a misallocation of funds. Sometime, I'll outline for you how the family foundation works.

ROOSTER. Don't spoil this.

MONICA. Your mom will be fine once she sees what this means—

IRENE. *(To **ROOSTER***)* Travel later in life or you'll get bored with it. *(Rises to leave)* I've got to have eye surgery. I can't see a dang thing.

OOZIE. Her eyes come and go. *(Hands her a cane.)*

IRENE. I can walk alone—

84

OOZIE. If she goes slowly.

(IRENE *slightly falls)*

MONICA. Mrs. Dubonnet?

IRENE. *(Shakes her head.)* Don't let that woman touch me!

*(***OOZIE** *and* **ROOSTER** *get* **IRENE** *up but she is very weak and has to lean against them.)*

ROOSTER. Lean on me.

IRENE. Someone's going to slip and sue me for a million dollars.

(IRENE *rests her head on* **ROOSTER** *and walks slowly out supported by* **OOZIE.** **MONICA** *watches them.* **BUNKY** *returns, chugging whiskey.)*

BUNKY. Everybody's gone? Lucky me.

MONICA. *(Keeping her voice low)* Wha'd you want?

BUNKY. One kiss. I'm so drunk I got mixed up and hollered for you in the street. Men are weak, sweetheart. What can I do? And women tempt us, you know...

MONICA. No closer.

BUNKY. You don't have to love me. It can be worth your while... *(Takes a few steps closer.)* One sweet dance... with a brother's hand...

MONICA. Go.

BUNKY. Bet you'd like to play with me. I like you. You know it. Women know it.

85

MONICA. No.

BUNKY. Don't be afraid.

MONICA. Stop.

BUNKY. But we have to taste each other first, and we can have a whole meal.

MONICA. Oh God. Move.

BUNKY. Kiss me. It won't kill you.

MONICA. No!

*(Leans her head back...***MONICA** *hits* **BUNKY.** *He storms about as if he'll beat her.)*

BUNKY. Most girls like it.

END OF SCENE 1

Also by
Rosary Hartel O'Neill...

The Awakening of Kate Chopin

Black Jack: The Thief of Possession

Degas in New Orleans

John Singer Sargent and Madame X

Marilyn/God

Property

Solitaire

Turtle Soup

Uncle Victor

White Suits in Summer

The Wings of Madness

Wishing Aces

Please visit our website **samuelfrench.com** for complete
descriptions and licensing information.

OTHER TITLES AVAILABLE FROM SAMUEL FRENCH

THE AWAKENING OF KATE CHOPIN

Rosary Hartel O'Neill

Full Length, Historical Drama / 2m, 2f

Kate Chopin, author of *The Awakening*, struggles to hold onto her marriage and her six small children as she launches her career as a novelist in 1884. Frustrating her attempts are: her wealthy next door neighbor, wanting to prove his masculinity; her jealous husband, stricken with malaria; the little sex-pot seamstress next door, the town gossip; and the bankrupt cotton business, which consumes all of her time. This crazy cacophony of personalities ends up compelling Kate toward her goal of becoming a famous author.

OTHER TITLES AVAILABLE FROM SAMUEL FRENCH

SOLITAIRE

Rosary Hartel O'Neill

Full Length, Southern Comedy / 3m, 2f / Interior

The Mississippi Gulf Coast estate of Irene Dubbonet is an unforgetable place to visit, but who would want to live there? All of her relatives, who hope to inherit it! This is a play about manipulation and what happens to family members' dreams when the odds are stacked against them. A cloud of doom hangs over Serenity Manor, until at last, virtue triumphs. Irene's son, the artist, Rooster, deeply anxious to prove himself, connives a scheme to help his "down and out" brother-in-law seize the estate. Funny situations sparked by witty lines bring the audience into an intriguing overview of topsy-turvy privileged life today.